Before reading

Look at the book cover together an~~d~~
Ask, "What do you think will ~~be~~

To build indepen~~dence~~   ~~read~~ed
at the start of this ~~book, read~~
back to pages 6 ~~and~~
the child.

During reading

Offer plenty of support ~~and~~ praise as the child reads the story.
Listen carefully and respond to events in the text.

In 9c, the new **Key Words** are not shown at the bottom of
the page. If the child hesitates over a word, turn to the back
of the book to practise reading it together. If the word is
phonically decodable, you can sound out the letters and
blend the sounds to read the word ("d-o-g, dog"). Praise the
child for their effort, then return to the story.

Pause every few pages and ask questions to check the child's
understanding of what they have read. If they begin to lose
concentration, stop reading and save the page for later.

Celebrate the child's achievement and come back to the
story the next day.

After reading

After reading this book, ask, "Did you enjoy the story? What did
you like about it?" Encourage the child to share their opinions.

Use the comprehension questions on page 54 to check the
child's understanding and recall of the text.

Ladybird

Series Consultant: Professor David Waugh
With thanks to Kulwinder Maude

LADYBIRD BOOKS

UK | USA | Canada | Ireland | Australia
India | New Zealand | South Africa

Ladybird Books is part of the Penguin Random House group of companies
whose addresses can be found at global.penguinrandomhouse.com.
www.penguin.co.uk   www.puffin.co.uk   www.ladybird.co.uk

Original edition of Key Words with Peter and Jane first published by Ladybird Books Ltd 1964
Series updated 2023
This book first published 2023
001

Text copyright © Ladybird Books Ltd, 1964, 2023
Illustrations by Martyn Cain
Based on characters and design by Gustavo Mazali
Illustrations copyright © Ladybird Books Ltd, 2023

With thanks to Liz Pemberton for her contributions in advising on the illustrations
With thanks to Inclusive Minds for connecting us with their Inclusion Ambassador network,
and in particular thanks to Guntaas Kaur Chugh for her input on the illustrations

Printed in China

The authorized representative in the EEA is Penguin Random House Ireland,
Morrison Chambers, 32 Nassau Street, Dublin D02 YH68

A CIP catalogue record for this book is available from the British Library

ISBN: 978-0-241-51099-5

All correspondence to:
Ladybird Books
Penguin Random House Children's
One Embassy Gardens, 8 Viaduct Gardens, London SW11 7BW

MIX
Paper from
responsible sources
FSC® C018179
FSC
www.fsc.org

Key Words

with Peter and Jane

9c

Back to school

Based on the original
Key Words with Peter and Jane
reading scheme and research by William Murray

Original edition written by William Murray
This edition written by James Clements
Illustrated by Martyn Cain
Based on characters and design by Gustavo Mazali

Peter and Jane were sorting out their things before going back to school.

"I am too big for my school clothes," Jane said.

"Me too!" said Peter.

"Could we buy some new ones?" Jane asked Mum.

"Yes, I think we should buy some new school things," said Mum.

"Peter, can you write down the things to buy as I call them out?" asked Mum. "We should get new jumpers that fit well, and you always want new socks and new pens for school."

"When we get back, could we go over to the park with my kite?" asked Peter.

"You may go to the park after you finish your homework for Mrs Rahim," said Mum.

At the shop, there were many children getting new school clothes.

"I wish we could go faster. We'll never get to the park!" said Peter.

"You never know," said Mum, "they could all get their clothes quickly."

Soon, they were in the shop. "That was fast!" said Peter. "You did say it might be."

Peter found a new jumper that fitted him well. Mum said they could buy it.

Jane put on a jumper, but it was too big. She put on another, but it was too tight. She could not fit it over her head!

"I'll never find a new jumper that fits," said Jane.

"Well," said Mum, "there is another place over the road we could go to."

They headed over the road to another shop. There were jumpers there that were just right.

Mum pulled out her money to buy the new jumper and some new socks too.

They walked back over the road to another shop to buy new pens.

"I think it's this way. This place always has good pens," said Mum.

Mum gave Peter and Jane some money to buy new pens. Jane found a big set of pens to buy with her money, but Peter was looking at kites.

"Peter, why are you over here looking at kites?" said Jane. "Your new red kite is at home, so I don't think you should buy another one! You should spend your money on pens."

Peter walked back over to the pens.

At home, Jane looked at her homework book.

"I will go and get my homework," said Peter. "Mrs Rahim gave us lots of spellings to learn."

Mum started to make dinner.

"I'm going to write about my new jumper in my homework book for Mr Bell," said Jane.

"Why don't you tell Mr Bell about the jumper that was too tight?" said Peter. "You could not get it over your head!"

"Why don't we take Peter's red kite to the park now?" asked Mum. "I have dinner cooking. We can eat it when Dad gets back."

Peter found his kite, and Tess found her ball.

On the way to the park, Jane saw a gold coin in the street.

"I found some money!" she said. "Should we keep it, Mum?"

"You did well to see that," said Mum. "Let's give the money away to help someone."

21

Peter had fun with his kite in the park. The wind was not blowing too fast.

Peter and Jane saw their friends Nish and Naz.

"I wish I had a kite like that. It is so fast!" said Nish.

"Please may I have a turn, Peter?" asked Naz.

Peter gave Naz a go with the kite before Mum called to say it was time to go back home for dinner.

23

The next day was Peter and Jane's first day back at school.

"May we walk with Will and Amber now?" asked Peter. He was in his new school jumper.

"Yes, let's go," said Dad.

"Could Amber come over for dinner after school, Dad?" asked Peter.

"I don't think she can come for dinner today," said Dad. "I think we may have another plan after school."

25

The children headed down their road, over another road and into school.

Peter walked to his teacher's class. He liked his teacher, Mrs Rahim.

Jane headed to another class with her teacher, Mr Bell.

"Please make your way in. Put your bags just over there," called the teachers.

27

"Sit in your places, please," called Mrs Rahim. Peter sat in a place near Amber.

Their teacher said they would learn about the sea that week. Peter was very pleased.

"My homework is all about my holiday at the sea!" Peter said to his friend.

29

In Jane's class, Mr Bell said the children should sit down in their places and place their homework books on their desks. Jane sat down near Will.

The teacher asked who would like to read their homework out to the class.

Jane's hand shot up very fast. "I would!" she said.

Peter was learning about animals that are found in the sea.

"Which animals would be found in a cold sea?" Mrs Rahim asked. "Why don't they get too cold?"

Peter looked in his book and read it very fast.

"I think I may have found out why, Mrs Rahim," said Peter.

"Good work, Peter!" said Mrs Rahim. "Could you just write it down in your book?"

Jane read out her homework. She read the part about Peter's kite landing in the sea and the part about Aunt Liz's very good dinners.

"Well, I think you had a good holiday, Jane!" said Mr Bell.

"I did," said Jane. "I always like holidays, but I like being back at school too."

After their lessons, the children headed out into the yard.

"What would you like to play, Peter?" asked Amber.

Peter found a ball. "Why don't we play football?" he said.

"We always play football!" said Amber. "Let's play another game. We never play catch."

"Good thinking," said Peter. "We should play catch."

After playtime, Jane and Will were in another part of the school. Will's dad, Tim, was their teacher for this lesson.

"Today, we will learn how to play the drums," said Mr Grant.

"I should never call my dad 'Dad' at school," said Will to Jane, "but I always forget."

"Could you all come and pick a drumstick?" called Mr Grant.

"Yes, Dad!" said Will.

In Peter's class, Mrs Rahim said, "Come in and sit in another place."

Peter quickly found a new place next to Naz. "I never get to sit next to Naz," he said.

Mrs Rahim asked them all to draw something from the sea.

"Why don't we draw some of the big fish from this book?" asked Peter.

"That could be good!" said Naz.

41

Jane and Will were waiting for their lunch.

"I would like some salad, please," Jane said.

"Me too," said Will.

"I wish you could come over for dinner at our house today," Jane said to Will.

"We could ask my dad. He could call your mum," said Will.

43

Will found his dad and asked him if he could go to Jane's house for dinner.

"I wish I could say yes," said Mr Grant, "but we have another plan for dinner today."

"But I would like to have dinner with Jane," said Will.

"Well, you never know," said his dad. "You may like this dinner plan more. Just wait and see!"

After lunch, Peter played football.

"You should just play with your feet in football," said Mrs Rahim. "Not your hands."

The children learned how to kick the ball into the goal. Peter kicked the ball really well, but one boy kicked the ball over the wall.

"Well, that was a big kick, Callum!" said Peter's teacher. "I will get the ball back."

47

Jane's teacher asked the class to write a story. Jane liked writing, and she could write very well.

Jane's story was about a boy who was given one wish. He wished for a new kite, but the wind blew his kite away over the road.

"I think I know who the boy is in that story!" said Mr Bell.

At the end of school, Peter and Jane walked back home with Dad.

"Well, what new things did you learn today?" Dad asked Peter.

"I learned about animals in the sea," Peter said.

"Did Mr Bell like your homework, Jane?" Dad asked.

"He did," said Jane.

When they were at their road, Dad turned the other way. Then they crossed over the next road.

"Why are we going this way, Dad?" asked Jane.

"This is the way to the park," said Peter.

At the park, Peter and Jane were surprised to see Will and Amber. They were there with their mum and little sister, Maya.

"We are all going to have a picnic dinner in the park!" said Dad.

"Yes!" said Peter and Jane. And they walked very fast to meet their friends.

Questions

Answer these questions about the story.

1 What new things do the children buy for school?

2 What does Jane find in the street on the way to the park?

3 What is Peter going to learn about at school this week?

4 Why do you think Will says that he should never call his dad "Dad" at school?

5 What is Jane's story about?

6 How does Dad surprise Peter and Jane at the end of the story?